EARLY CLASSIC SERIES

LITTLE AGGIE'S FRESH SNOWDROPS

AND

LITTLE VIOLET

ORIGINALLY PUBLISHED IN 1871

F.M.S.

ISBN: 978-1-941213-21-6

Cover design and layout: Violet Hershberger
Illustrations: Josephine Beachy

Printed in the USA

Published by:
TGS International
P.O. Box 355
Berlin, Ohio 44610 USA
Phone: 330-893-4828
Fax: 330-893-2305
www.tgsinternational.com

TGS000857

LITTLE AGGIE'S FRESH SNOWDROPS

AND

LITTLE VIOLET

TWO TALES FOR THE YOUNG

By F.M.S., author of
Hope On and *King Jack of Haylands*

ORIGINALLY PUBLISHED IN

LONDON

BY

T. NELSON AND SONS, PATERNOSTER ROW;
EDINBURGH; AND NEW YORK.

1871

CONTENTS

LITTLE AGGIE'S FRESH SNOWDROPS
AND WHAT THEY DID IN ONE DAY

Whatsoever things are pure,
whatsoever things are lovely . . .
think on these things.
Philippians 4:8

I love the little snowdrop flower,
The first in all the year,
Without a stain upon its leaf,
So snowy white and clear.
For pure of heart, and innocent,
And teachable, and mild,
And modest in its ways and words,
Should be a Christian child.

WHERE THE SNOWDROPS
CAME FROM

Who could describe their loveliness as they grew on that woodland bank? The sun shone with as much warmth as it is in the habit of giving on cold February days, and the snowdrops seemed to think it was high time to come out of their cold, damp beds and tell of the other flowers that were to follow them by and by. It was as if they said, "It has been very dull and dreary lately, and you might almost fancy that we were all dead, but here we come to teach you to be more trustful and hopeful about the good things the future has in store for you."

And there they were, amidst the damp, glistening, creeping ivy, the mossy grass, and the long, waving fern leaves which were still fresh and green in spite of the snow, frost, and constant rains of the winter. Each snowdrop stood by itself in its spotless, dazzling whiteness, looking most truly as if the snow had left a legacy behind it in the shape of their pure little blossoms.

But it was not on that woodland bank that their lives were to be spent, for before the sun had been up an hour, and when they were just opening their folded petals, a little hand, red with cold and thin with want, grasped their slight green stalks. It was Aggie, a little girl from the great town about three miles off. She was very hungry, and so were her baby brothers and sisters, for her poor, sick mother had no food to give them for breakfast. So Aggie

had gotten up very early and come over to this wood to gather them, that she might sell them and earn a few pence to get a loaf of bread. She had brought along Paul, her little brother, more to get

3

him out of Mother's way than anything else; but Paul thought he was very useful in pointing out to Aggie where the snowdrops grew.

To him it was only play, but to his sister, who knew that those white blossoms were to bring food to starving creatures, it was real, life-and-death earnest.

"Stay, Paul, stay," she cried. "You tread on them. Yes, I see they grow thickly up there. Stay where you are;" and with nimble feet Aggie sprang up higher on the bank and gathered them quickly. It was strange to see the eager look on that starved, pinched face as she stretched her cold hand from one flower to another. She was dressed in rags; the large bonnet on her head was her mother's, and almost smothered her pale face. Her bones were all distinctly marked, for there was very little flesh to conceal them, and there was an old, careworn look about her, which would have made one believe it

4

impossible that she was only nine years old. But it was true, nevertheless, for it was under the hand of that keenest of sharpeners for the wits—grim poverty—that Aggie had been trained.

"Me tired, Aggie, me tired. Me want summat to eat!" cried Paul from the bottom of the bank.

"Well, I've got enough now," said Aggie, turning around with her pinafore full. Now, Paul, we'll sit down on this log and settle them." And down she clambered, only stopping to break off some little sprigs from the boxwood trees she passed.

"Now, you can help," she said smilingly, showing him her treasures. "You can help tie them up, Paul," and she drew from the bosom of her dress a ball of gray worsted and set to work. In a half hour she had a dozen bunches, done up with a sprig of the dark green boxwood at the back of each, setting off the whiteness of the snowdrops.

"Come, Paul. Now you'll have a nice, good

breakfast. Come along to the shops, and we'll get some money," she said cheerfully as she settled her flowers in an old broken basket and held out her hand to the little boy by her side. Then they crossed the brook which bounded the coppice, and ran through the fields beyond it until they reached the high road.

For some time Paul got on very well, but by degrees the hardness of the road made his feet ache. Aggie, perceiving that he dragged her hand very much, looked at him and saw that he was crying bitterly.

She knew it was hunger that made him cry, for he was generally a brave little fellow. Stopping instantly, she put her arms around him, saying, "Don't cry, Paul, don't, dear; we'll soon be back."

"I do want summat to eat, I do—I do," sobbed Paul. "And I tired—I sick—Aggie, I so sick."

Poor Aggie was tired too, but she did not think

6

of herself. She laid the basket on the ground and took the heavy boy in her arms, wrapped her ragged shawl around him, and gave him the snowdrops to hold. Thus she staggered on under his weight, but though her arms and back ached, and though she could only breathe with difficulty under her heavy burden, no word of discontent passed her lips. With cheering, patient words she brightened her brother's face, until at length he said he was rested and would "walk a bit."

At last they had reached the great town and were walking through the crowded, bustling streets. The moisture in the woods had glistened beautifully on the leaves, moss, and ferns and had hung in drops from the flowers, but here in the city, it was mixed with dirt and dust to make mud everywhere. The snowdrops looked purer than ever when contrasted with the blackness and grimness of things around them.

WHERE THE SNOWDROPS CAME FROM

"Fresh snowdrops, two bunches for three half-pence," said Aggie, popping her head into a large fruiterer's shop and holding out her basket.

"You're too late—we have plenty for today—be off with you," said the shopkeeper gruffly, and Aggie withdrew with a disappointed face.

"Look, Aggie, what good buns," said little Paul, pointing to a stand at the door of a shop. "Me'd like one so much."

Aggie thought she would too. No one was standing by the buns. She could easily slip a couple under her shawl. She drew near to them for that purpose when suddenly there rushed into her mind the thought, *God says, "Thou shalt not steal."* Quickly she pulled Paul on.

"Why didn't you take one?" he asked fretfully.

"Because it would have been naughty, Paul. We mustn't take what isn't ours."

"Why not? We hungry," said little Paul, looking

up with tearful eyes.

"Yes, but God will take care of us," said Aggie, bravely trying to force her own quivering lips into a smile. "Paul, don't you know that before we went out, Mother made us pray to our heavenly Father 'to give us this day our daily bread?' If we steal it, it isn't His giving it, is it?"

"No," said Paul, "but I think He's forgot."

"No, no, He hasn't. It was He who put the thought about the snowdrops into my head this morning, and it was He who made 'em grow, and He'll make the people buy 'em too." Aggie paused to hold out a bunch to a young lady who was passing and said, "Fresh snowdrops miss—so fresh, picked only this morning."

"I don't want them," said the young lady, but she smiled as she spoke.

Aggie liked the lady's smile almost as much as if she had bought her flowers. It seemed to help her go on. It was an encouragement and a ray of comfort to her poor aching heart. But Aggie was too late that morning. Though she wandered wearily up and down the streets, no one seemed to want her snowdrops. All the shops seemed to be supplied. Her hopes began to die away, her cheeks to become paler and more wan, and her little brother was crying piteously for food.

"Kind gentlemen, do buy my fresh snowdrops! Fresh snowdrops—quite fresh," she said earnestly to a party of young men who came gaily along the street. But they took no notice except to brush rudely past her, and in so doing they upset her basket. In an instant the pure white blossoms were lying on the dirty wet pavement.

Aggie did not scream; she only sat down mournfully on a step close by, covered her face with her hands, and burst into tears while Paul picked up the flowers. Alas! They were no longer white. Every bunch had some in it which were quite spoiled, and all Aggie's hopes of their procuring a breakfast for the hungry ones at home were quite at an end.

"What's the matter, little one? What's all this

crying about?" asked a kindly voice beside her.

"These gemmen—if they calls themselves such— knocked over her basket, and her snowdrops fell in the mud," said a good-natured boy, helping Paul to pick them up.

"They're spoilt! They're spoilt, and we shall have no breakfast!" sobbed Aggie.

"Poor child, you look as if you wanted it too," said the woman who had spoken first. "Are the snowdrops quite spoiled?"

"Yes, every bunch has some dirt on it, and some of 'em got trampled on," replied the little girl with a fresh burst of tears.

"Well, but all the flowers aren't spoiled. Look, my dear, some of them have only a little spot on one or two of the blossoms. The middle ones are clean, and they're the freshest, nicest snowdrops I've seen today."

Aggie looked up more brightly. The good woman

spoke so kindly, and her face was so pleasant, it quite comforted her. Her tears went away altogether when her new friend drew a bright sixpence from her pocket and said, "Here, my dear, two of these bunches are quite good for nothing, but I'll give you this for the rest, if you like."

There is no need to tell how gratefully Aggie took the offer, and then she and Paul put the soiled snowdrops back into the basket, knowing that the little ones at home would delight in them.

A few minutes after, they were in a baker's shop buying a big loaf, and then they set off at a quick run towards the house, where they were so eagerly expected.

"Paul," said Aggie as they trotted along, "I told you God would take care of us. Mother said He would. We prayed for bread, and look at the big loaf He's given us."

"If I was a growed-up man, Aggie, I'd get cake,

not bread—cake, like what's in the windows."

"I think bread's very good," said Aggie contentedly as she hugged the big loaf closer to her.

"If we had lots of money, we'd be quite happy," said little Paul musingly.

"No, not *quite,*" said Aggie, laying emphasis on the last word, as if she knew it would go a long way towards making them so.

"Not quite, you know, Paul, unless Daddy had come back from sea. That makes Mother look so sad and pale. Thinking of Daddy makes her start and shiver when the wind howls against the window. Oh, I wish, I wish he'd come! He doesn't know how hungry we are."

By this time they had reached the narrow court where they lived. Entering the dingy lodging house, the top rooms of which they occupied, they toiled up the steep stairs on weary feet.

"Mother, here's bread—here's a loaf!" cried little

Aggie, bursting into their room. "We shan't starve now!" But before she could say another word, she was clasped in a strong pair of arms, and a loving, hearty voice was saying, "My little brave lass, God bless her!" and Aggie's cheek was covered with her father's kisses.

The ship had come that morning into port, and he had been paid, so here he was, with money enough to save them all from beggary.

"Come, Aggie, child, get me some breakfast. I'm hungry," he exclaimed after he had tossed Paul nearly up to the ceiling and brought the color back into his pale cheeks. Afterwards they all declared that bread had never before tasted so good as that which had been bought with Aggie's fresh snowdrops.

CHAPTER TWO

SNOWDROPS IN THE BACK PARLOR AND THE SHOP WINDOW

Having brought our little Aggie into smooth waters, let us follow her snowdrops to their new abode. The good-natured woman who had bought them kept a green-grocer's shop in a retired street at some little distance, but she walked briskly and soon reached it.

"Susan," she asked cheerfully as she entered the door, "hasn't Billy taken those potatoes to No. 9? He must run directly, and you must abide there a few minutes longer."

"Oh, Mother," answered the little girl behind the counter, "Jamie's so fretful this morning. He says his side is so bad, and he's crying so dreadful."

"Poor little man! Well, I'll go and see if I can't comfort him a bit," answered his mother, a sad shade crossing her brow at the mention of her little, suffering, crippled boy. With that, she entered the back parlor behind the shop.

A boy of about eleven years old, very much deformed, was sitting in a low chair by the fire, his face thin and pale.

"Come, Jamie, man, what's the matter?" asked his mother in her own bright, cheery voice as she came to his side.

A long fit of sobbing was the little boy's only answer.

"Jamie, love, this mustn't be. Tell Mammy what it is," she said tenderly as she knelt down by him.

"Oh, the pain, the pain! I'm so tired," and the

little pale face rested on her shoulder.

"Well, Jamie, it'll make it worse to cry," said his mother, folding her arms around him and stroking his fair hair. "That's not all that's the matter, my boy; you don't often cry for pain, laddie."

"It isn't only pain," he sobbed, "but, oh, Mother, Billy's been talking to me."

"And how has he vexed you, my boy?"

"He says—oh, Mother—he says that you spend all your money on the doctor for me."

"Shame, shame!" said his mother. "He should know better than to say such things."

"And, Mother, I'm so useless. I waste all your money, they say, yet I do nothing at all to help you."

"Yes, you do, my child, when you're bright and happy."

"Oh, I wish, I *wish* God would let me die," sobbed the little fellow.

"Hush, hush, Jamie, love," said his mother, drawing him close to herself. "Hush, God won't be pleased to hear His little child speak so fretfully."

"I'm not fretful," said Jamie.

"Just a little bit, I think, dear," whispered his

mother. "Is it because you love the Lord Jesus so much that you want to be with Him up in heaven? Is that why you want to die?"

"No," he answered in low, ashamed tones. "It's because I'm tired and don't like all this pain."

"And yet it's God who sends the pain, my darling. So it is a little fretful to cry out about it so much, isn't it?"

"Yes."

"Will you ask Him to make you patient until He comes to take you to His happy home, where you'll be strong and well?"

"Yes, Mother."

"There's my own dear boy. And now you are going to do some work for me. Look at these snowdrops in my basket. I want you to take out all the dirty ones and tie the clean ones up again with some fresh green. That will be useful, and then I can sell them, and you'll have earned some money for me."

Jamie's face brightened, and he watched eagerly while his mother drew up his little chair to the table and laid the basket, some twine, and a pair of scissors before him.

"Oh, the pretty things, Mother! What beauties they are! Where did you get 'em?"

Then his mother told him their story and how they had purchased a breakfast for the poor little children.

Jamie looked up thoughtfully from his work of sorting the stained flowers and said, "Mother, they're worse off than me; I had some breakfast."

"Yes, dear, thank God you had. Now I must go to the shop, and you'll be a good, patient little lad, won't you?"

"Yes, Mother; and may I have the snowdrops I pick out, because some of them are still white?"

"You may, dear, and put them in your mug with 'James' on it."

And then the little lame boy was left alone with the snowdrops.

Quickly and skillfully, his small, thin fingers sorted them and tied them up afresh, while his eyes, tired with crying, were refreshed with the sight of their pure whiteness. Before long his work was finished, and then he sat with his little elbows resting on the table, looking at the bunches of flowers and wondering at their beauty.

"I wonder why God made the snowdrops," he said to himself at last. "It must have been a great deal of trouble. I wonder what they are good for?"

"To brighten us all up by the sight of 'em, to be sure," said his sister Susan, who had just come into the room and heard what he was saying. With that, she ran up the stairs with her duster.

Jamie gave a sigh as he heard her bounding steps, but her words seemed quite to answer his question. "They don't do any good, and yet God thought it worthwhile to make them just for people to look at. Well, then, perhaps He thought it worthwhile to make me for that also. Yet I can't be for them to look at, because I'm a hunchback, and it wouldn't do 'em a bit of good to see me. I don't know though, since Mother says it cheers her up when I've got a bright face and a cheery smile. I know what I'll do. I'll ask God, who made the snowdrops, to make me of some use too. Oh, I wish I were pure and white like them! If ever I'm like them at all, I shall only be a poor little dirty one. Well, even they are little bright things to me in my mug, and I know what can make my heart as pure as the purest of them. I'll ask for that."

And little Jamie prayed to his Father in heaven, and asked to be shown how he might be useful, and patient, and do his work, and that his heart might be washed from all its sins and made pure in the blood of the Saviour.

When Jamie's mother came in, she found him sitting quietly at the table, reading one of his little books, and he greeted her with a bright smile. She praised his nosegays, pulled out two or three very pure blossoms, and put them into his mug. Then she went back into the shop, asking him to watch over his little sisters, Jane and Bessie, when they came home from the infant school, whither Billy had gone to fetch them.

They soon arrived, their little cheeks glowing with the quick run and their little tongues going very fast indeed. Jamie would rather have been left alone in quiet. He was a thoughtful little fellow, and his ill health made him even more so than boys of his age generally are. He liked nothing better than to be left alone to think and read and fancy things for himself. But this was not the usefulness which he longed for that morning, and the snowdrops doing their lowly work of brightening others had taught him a lesson.

"Hush, Jenny," said little Bessie, pulling her sister into a far corner of the room. "Billy says Jamie's as cross as the cats this morning. Let's play with dolly over here."

Jamie heard the words, and they made him even unhappier than he had been before, but he did not speak. He only watched the two little girls at their whispered play and sighed to think how much they feared and disliked him. For some time the game went on merrily enough, but then Jamie heard a cry of anger from Bessie. Looking up to discover the cause, he saw that Jenny was trying to pull the doll away from her by force, and that its arm had been broken off in the fray. Bessie's first thought was to revenge the doll's fracture by dealing vigorous blows on Jenny's head, but then real sorrow for her dear dolly became mixed with her anger, and she sat down with it in her arms and cried most piteously.

On other days, Jamie would have spoken pettishly and told her to be quiet, but he remembered his wish to be useful, and so he said gently and kindly, "What's the matter, little woman?"

"Naughty Jenny broke my doll! Me'll beat her, and me'll tell Mother. Me'll…."

At this Jenny began to whimper. Jamie began to fear that he could not give much comfort, but he was determined to try, so he called out again, "Come here, Bessie, and bring Miss Dolly. I'll be the doctor and examine her arm."

"No, me'll go into the shop to Mother and tell her."

Jamie knew that this was just what his mother did not wish, so he said very kindly, "Do bring it here, Bessie. I'm so sorry for poor dolly, and so's Jenny. I see it in her face."

Bessie came over hesitatingly and laid the doll on his knee. Then Jamie pretended to be the doctor and gave his opinion in such a grand voice that Jenny laughed, and something like a smile came over Bessie's tearful face.

"Now, I'll bind up her arm if you'll give me a little bit of tape," said Jamie.

Jenny brought it to him, and in a few minutes the doll was mended. The doctor, with a wise shake of his head, pronounced the patient out of danger.

"Good Jamie," said Bessie. "You very kind and nice, not one bit like the cross pussy cats."

Jamie smiled. It was pleasant to hear this simple praise, though it was given by a little girl only five years old.

"Now, Jenny and Bessie, shall we make a feast in honor of Miss Dolly getting well?" he asked brightly. The little ones were all smiles directly and watched with eager delight while he cut out paper plates and dishes, divided an orange and some bread into small pieces, and placed his mug

of snowdrops in the center of the feast.

About an hour after, when his mother came in to prepare dinner, he greeted her with a bright smile, and the two little girls cried out, "Mother, Mother, Jamie's made boo'ful plates, and we so happy. Jamie not cross this morning."

Mrs. Grey bent down to kiss him and whispered, "Thank you, my boy. You have helped me very much today."

In the course of the evening, Jamie's mother came in for a moment from the shop, and laying down three bright pennies before him, she said, "There, Jamie, that's for you, for your own. I've sold all the snowdrops: three bunches to a young lady, who looked so pleased to get them, and a factory girl took another. And have you had a nice day, my little son?"

"Yes, Mother, quite happy."

"And have you forgiven Billy?"

"Yes, Mother, long ago. I was very cross to him."

"There's my own Jamie. Now I'm going out to get the marketing for tomorrow, and Susan's going to put the little ones to bed."

Jamie sat alone by the fire for some time. He did not care to light the candle his mother had left by his side, but sat looking into the glowing coals and watching the firelight dancing on the floor, on the window, across which the little curtain was drawn, and on the table where his mug of snowdrops stood. They looked purer and more beautiful than ever in the flickering light, and little Jamie's heart was full of pleasant thoughts about them and about the happy day he had spent in trying to be of some use in the world.

After a little while Billy came stealing in. Jamie noticed directly that something was the matter with him. He felt quite certain of it when he saw him come up to the chimney piece and stand there silently, sometimes raising his jacket sleeve and rubbing it across his eyes.

"What's the matter, Billy?" he asked at length.

"I've hurt my hand," Billy replied gruffly.

"How?"

"I've cut it on a bit of glass."

"Is it very bad?"

"Yes."

Jamie was very sorry, but Billy's tone was so discouraging that he did not know what more to say, so for some time neither of them spoke. At last Jamie ventured again, "Billy, may I tie a bit of rag around your hand?"

"Yes, if you will."

Jamie lighted the candle, and Billy brought over the rag and some cotton; then Jamie bathed the cut and tied the rag around it. "Are you going to the night school, Billy?" he asked when he had finished.

"No," said Billy, coloring and turning away

32

towards the fire again.

Jamie hesitated. He knew it was wrong for Billy to not go, yet he feared to say anything to his brother. His sense of right gained the victory, however, and he asked gently, "Hadn't you better go, Billy? Mother won't be pleased."

A deep sob was Billy's only answer.

"What is it, Billy? Oh, do tell me!" cried Jamie, thoroughly distressed.

"Oh, Jamie, Jamie, what shall I do?" cried Billy. "I've been a bad, bad boy, and I daren't tell Mother, and I daren't go to school."

"What is it?" said Jamie fearfully.

"Why, you know, Mother gave me three pence to pay my week's schooling last night, and I fell to playing pitch-and-toss with Joe Robinson and lost it all; and now, what shall I do?"

"Oh, Billy, I'm so sorry."

"So am I, and I feel so bad; but, oh, Jamie, I can't

go to school tonight."

A quick rush of thought filled Jamie's mind. There was a battle between his own pleasure and Billy's welfare, but he was helped. Putting his hand in his little pocket, he drew out the three bright pence his mother had given him, and holding them out to Billy, he said, "Here's these. You can have them; but you'll promise to tell Mother all about it, won't you?"

"Yes," whispered Billy. "I can't go to bed till I have. But, Jamie, I don't like taking this."

"Oh, do take them; then I shall feel they're of some good. Now, it's time for you to be off."

Billy rose and got down his cap, but he came back for a minute to say, "Jamie, I'll not speak to you again like I did this morning if you'll be always jolly and bright as you've been today."

"Jolly and bright!" They were comforting words to little Jamie. God had thought it worthwhile to make him, and now he had found out the reason. From that day, instead of living a useless, selfish life, he became the brightener of the back parlor, having cheerful smiles and loving words for those about him, and doing many little kind, useful actions which helped others and made himself happier. The lesson of the snowdrops had not been thrown away upon the little lame boy who lived behind the shop.

CHAPTER THREE

SNOWDROPS IN THE BIRTHDAY WREATH

Edith Clifford was the young lady who had seen the snowdrops in Mrs. Grey's window. She had searched vainly in the principal shops for some that looked fresh and pure, and had been greatly delighted at discovering these when she was returning home.

She carried them carefully and soon reached a house in a quiet terrace where several little faces peeped out of the parlor window, eagerly awaiting her arrival.

"Here's Edith, and she's got some flowers!" cried a host of merry voices.

"Yes, I've got them, and now we shall see what a pretty wreath they make. Freddy, will you get

me some of the prettiest bits of ivy you can find in the garden?"

A handsome, laughing boy bounded off at her words, and a little girl of eight years old, with a happy face and glossy black hair, came to Edith's side to admire the snowdrops.

"Are they for me, Edith?" she whispered, touching the pure white petals softly.

"Yes, darling, for your birthday wreath. I thought you would like these better than anything else."

"Much better. Papa loves them so much."

"Well, Mary, I am going to make the wreath of ivy, and then the snowdrops will peep out here and there from under the dark green leaves."

"Beautiful, beautiful!" said little Mary, clapping her hands "And then I shall wear it this evening at my party, shan't I, Edith?"

"Yes, darling. Look, here comes Fred with the ivy," and soon Edith's nimble fingers were twisting the graceful wreath.

"Run along now, Mary. You know the party is to begin at half past five. You must go change your frock and have your black locks combed into some order. What have you been about all this afternoon?"

"Oh, Fred and Charlie and I have been making a house amongst the curtains. Then nurse's little girl, Ellen, came in and saw us, and played with us. She's such a dear little thing, Edith, so shy and pretty."

"Well, run off now and get ready," and then Edith went on with her wreath in peace.

It was soon finished, and when she had tied up the remaining snowdrops with a little bow of green ribbon and laid them and the wreath on the table spread with Mary's presents, she left the room. She returned in time to crown her little sister when she came back with smooth hair and a clean white frock.

"There, little woodland beauty," said Edith merrily as she stood off at a little distance to see the effect of her handiwork. "That wreath makes you more beautiful than ever. Look, Charlie, don't the snowdrops look beautiful?"

"Very!" said a deep voice beside her, and two strong arms were thrown around Mary, making her a prisoner.

"Oh, Papa, Papa!" she cried. "How do you like my wreath?"

"More than any wreath I have ever seen, my little Mary. Edith seems to have remembered my fancy for snowdrops."

"They are Mary's own particular flowers, Papa," said Edith, smiling. "She was born just when they were coming into blossom."

"Yes—she was," said Mr. Clifford with a sigh, for he remembered that on that day, eight years ago, when Mary and the snowdrops were just entering upon life, Mary's mama had died. But he did not wish that his little girl's happy evening should be clouded with sorrowful thoughts, so he only drew her into his arms and kissed her once or twice, and then he turned away.

"Oh, Papa, you'll come to my party, won't you?"

"Yes, love, I will come in by and by for a game, but I must go and visit a poor sick boy now." Mr. Clifford was a clergyman, and he was so much engaged with his parish work that he could very seldom spare time for play, and it was in consequence one of the greatest treats that his children could have.

"Edith, dear, you will take care of the little folks, won't you?"

"Yes, Papa," answered Edith, who, being several years older than Mary, was always looked upon by her as a mother, the only mother she had ever known. Certainly it would have been difficult for any mother to give Mary a more warm and devoted love than Edith did.

And now the party began as troops of merry little faces and gay dresses filled the room. Edith and Mary went amongst their guests, welcoming them and trying to set them at ease. A large and substantial tea did this better than anything else, and by the time it was over, the little tongues were going fast enough and everybody was ready for games. Mary was queen of the evening and chose "post" for the first game. When they were tired of this, Edith, in her famous style, told them a story of the grandmother's coach. She kept the guests all whirling round and round and making such a commotion that Fred said he wondered the poor grandmother's nerves were not shaken to pieces, with all the smacking of the whip, the starting of the horses, the barking of the little dog, the banging of the doors, and the creaking of the wheels. But everyone laughed very much over it and pronounced Edith to be a capital storyteller.

Blindman's-buff came next, and Mr. Clifford entered the room in the middle of it. A cry of pleasure burst from the whole party at his entrance, a crowd of little hands stretched out to him, and loving faces looked up to greet him. He spoke to them all kindly and then allowed the blind man in the middle the pleasure of catching him, and he was blindfolded in his stead. Then he kept the children in a continual state of excitement by the long swoops he made across the room. They dodged down under his arms and ran laughing over to the other side. When they had all thoroughly tired themselves, Mr. Clifford, for a change in activity, puzzled them completely with funny questions.

But though all was seemingly joyful and full of mirth, there was a dark cloud on one little face. Mr. Clifford's quick eye was not long in discovering it

on none other than his own little Mary. He took no notice of it until the last little guest had departed, the last good night was said, and the two boys were discussing with Edith the delights of the evening.

Then Mr. Clifford went over to the window where Mary was sitting with her wreath in her hand, looking very disconsolately on its faded blossoms.

"Well, little woman, has this been a pleasant evening?" he said gently, laying his hand on her head.

"Yes, Papa, pretty well."

"Only 'pretty well'?"

Mary shook her head, but did not speak.

Her father stood by her side for a few minutes, expecting her to say something more, but she did not, so he went away to his study.

He had not been there long before there came a little timid knock at his door, and Mary entered.

"I've come to say good night, Papa." But she did not raise her face to his with its usual merry smile. She only hung down her head and looked very sad.

"What is the matter, dear Mary?" he asked gravely as he put his arm around her. Her only answer was to lay her head on his shoulder and burst into tears.

"You are tired, dear—tired of all this play. Go to bed, and sleep it off. You will be your own little self again tomorrow."

"No, no, Papa, it isn't that."

"Well, what is it then?"

"I don't like to have only this wreath that withers away, Papa. Julia Desmond told me that *she* wouldn't wear paltry snowdrops that would die in one evening. Her mama gave her a lovely wreath on her birthday, all of white artificial flowers and silver leaves, and she keeps it now put away in a bandbox. And here, you see, mine are only real flowers that can die. And then, Papa, I showed her my presents, and the paint box you gave me, and the boys' book, and Edith's doll. But she said that she had been given a much bigger paint box, and the book was bad print, and that *her* doll's eyes opened and shut. She supposed you couldn't afford those kind of things for me. And then she asked me what I had done all day; and when I told her, she laughed and said she wondered how I could have pleasure in playing with a little poor child—she always went for a drive in the park or something. And, Papa, just then Edith came up and told me that Ellen was waiting for some of my birthday cake in the hall. I was ashamed Julia should see her, because she was so shabby, and so I said, 'Let her wait.' "

"Oh, Mary, I am so sorry." Her father's grieved look told even more than his words.

"Well, Papa, it was too vexing."

"What was too vexing, Mary—Julia's folly, or your wicked pride?"

"No, Papa, it was all vexing—the wreath and everything."

"Your pretty wreath, that pleased you so much! Mary, I do not think you had any right to wear those snowdrops."

"Why not, Papa?"

"Because they are humble little flowers, and my little Mary is not humble."

"Am I not, Papa?"

"No." And her father spoke sorrowfully in a very grave voice.

Mary was silent for a few minutes, but then, throwing her arms around him, she sobbed out, "Papa, Papa, I see it now, and that's what has been making me so unhappy—not the things themselves, but my old wicked pride. No, I was not fit to have the pretty snowdrops. Oh, Papa, how shall I be humble?"

"There is but one way, my darling. Learn from Him who was 'meek and lowly in heart,' and ask Him to take the naughty pride from your heart. Then by and by I shall see my little girl, like the snowdrops, ready to take the place which God means for her and to fill that place in the way that

50

best pleases Him, with loving humility. If the dear little white snowdrops can teach my Mary this, I do not think her birthday wreath will be as perishable as Julia Desmond's artificial flowers."

"What do you mean, dear Papa? Julia's wreath can never fade."

"No, but the white will soil, the silver will tarnish, and Julia will throw the old wreath away. Yours, my child, will be an everlasting one, for if the snowdrops teach you humility and contentment, they will be always blossoming in your heart. Do you understand me, or are you too sleepy?"

"No, Papa, I think I understand."

"That's right. Then let this new year be a wiser and a humbler one than last."

"I'll try, Papa, and I'll ask to be taught to be more humble. And, Papa dear, Ellen shall have all the rest of my birthday cake."

"I don't know what Charlie and Fred would say

to that, dear," said Mr. Clifford, laughing.

Mary colored. "Very well, Papa. Then Ellen shall have all my share. I will take it to her, and I will try not to wish for any when I see Charlie and Fred eating theirs."

Mr. Clifford answered by a loving kiss of approval, and then she went away to bed. When she was gone, Mr. Clifford saw two or three of the snowdrops, which had dropped from the birthday wreath, lying on the ground. He took them up and placed them within the leaves of one of his books. Years afterwards, when Mary had learned the lessons of humility and contentment much more fully than her father had dared to hope she ever would, he showed her the withered blossoms and said gently, "Mary, my child, your snowdrops were everlastings." Mary only smiled in answer, for she knew well what he meant.

CHAPTER FOUR

WHERE THE SNOWDROPS LAY IN THE EVENING

To know where the snowdrops lay in the evening, we must follow the factory girl who had bought the last bunch of snowdrops in Mrs. Grey's window. Her name was Alice Mansfield, and her home was in a dark and dingy court. It was but a poor home—a lonely room, up four pairs of stairs. Alice often thought of the happy country home which she had been obliged to leave. She longed for one breath of country air or one glance at a country scene.

But this evening she had put away her gloomy thoughts and was looking forward to giving someone else pleasure.

When she reached home and had hung up her bonnet and shawl, she carried her bunch of snowdrops to the room next to her own and knocked at the door.

"Come in," said a mournful voice, and she entered the room.

It was more comfortable than her own. There were marks in it which seemed to betoken that its owners had known better times. A woman whose face bore marks of anxiety, sorrow, and want was wearing a widow's cap and sitting beside a bed where a little nine-year-old boy was lying. His small face was wasted and pale, save for a bright and burning spot on each of his cheeks. His breathing was hurried and difficult, his thin hands were stretched beside him, and his dark brown hair

strayed over the pillow. His large eyes gleamed with a lustrous light, though the dullness of death was already coming upon them. As he caught sight of Alice in the doorway, he smiled faintly, and his whole face brightened as she brought the snowdrops to his side.

"Thank you—oh, thank you," he whispered. "Will you put them in water?"

"Yes. Where is your glass?"

His mother brought it, and Alice wondered at the calm of her face. She did not know that it was sent from heaven.

"How is he?" whispered Alice as the mother came near.

"Worse. This is the last I may have of him," she answered. "Mr. Clifford has been here praying beside him."

"Alice, stoop down," said little Willie suddenly. She obeyed.

"I love those flowers. They are beautiful. They're like what Mr. Clifford has been telling me."

"What's that, Willie?"

"Those who have washed their robes—go on, Mother."

She took up his words and added softly, " 'And made them white in the blood of the Lamb, therefore are they before the throne of God.' "

"Yes, that's it," said Willie. "I'm going up to Jesus. I love those flowers because they mind me of Him. Mother, sing to me. Sing 'Around the Throne.' "

In a trembling voice the poor mother complied, and Alice sat and listened as tears rolled down her cheeks. She had no friends in that great city except little Willie and his mother, and now Willie was going away from her, leaving her with a great feeling of loneliness in her heart. Ever since she had known him, it had been something to which she could look forward during her hard day's work—those pleasant evening visits to Mrs. Elder's room and Willie's sick bed. She was always contriving little pleasures of some kind for him. The little boy was very fond of her, and his mother loved her for her good nature and kindness to him.

And now, as Alice looked at the fair small face on which death's hand was busy, her heart sank at the thought of parting with him, for she knew but little of the joys to which he was going.

"Alice, don't ye cry," said Willie feebly, laying his thin hand on hers. "Don't cry because I'm going away; you'll come too with Mother, won't you? And I'll watch at the gate for you."

"Oh, Willie, Willie, don't go!" sobbed poor Alice as tears ran down her rough face.

"I must, Alice, because He's calling," and a smile of beaming joy passed over the face of the little boy. "And I'm 'to walk with him in white.' Oh, Alice, it's so happy!"

Alice's tears fell faster, and she feared she might distress him; so, asking his mother to call her if she wanted her, she stooped down and kissed the little face she loved so well, saying, "Good night, dear Willie."

"Good night," he whispered. "Think of me when you see the snowdrops—I love them so. And don't grieve, Alice, because I'm walking with Him in white."

"Good night," and then she went down to her own little room and prayed to the Saviour—prayed as she had not done for years, and rose strengthened and calmed. Then, wearied out by hard work and grief of heart, she lay down and slept soundly.

About midnight she was wakened by Mrs. Elder's voice beside her. "Come up and see him," she whispered. "Come and see what is left of him, for he himself is walking in white before the throne of God." The mother's heart was wrung with sorrow too deep for words, and silently she led the way into her room.

There lay the little boy as if asleep. His eyes were closed, his breathing had ceased, a smile was on his

white lips, and the snowdrops were lying on his breast, his thin hands clasped upon them.

"Those snowdrops were the last pleasure he had, Alice. He smiled on them the last thing," said his mother.

"Oh, Mrs. Elder, he looks like a verse I learned long ago at school: 'Blessed are the pure in heart, for they shall see God.' "

"He sees God now," said the mother. "But, oh, Alice, I'm lonely. I have no child."

"Let me be your daughter," said Alice tenderly. "Do let me."

"Yes, my child. You loved my Willie, and you will love me."

"I will—I do! Oh, if I could but comfort you?"

"God will do that," said the mother, looking tenderly down on little Willie. Then she added, "He only can."

And now the snowdrops' day was ended. The

darkness of night was spread like a mantle over the city and over the wood where they had grown in the morning. The work of the little white flowers was done; they had cheered, brightened, and comforted some of the toiling children of earth. They had lighted up dark places and brought thoughts of peace and joy to sorrowful hearts. They had reminded some of the better hope beyond them, of the purity of "the land which is very far off," and of the happiness of those who have put off their earth-stained dresses, to whom the words of promise are fulfilled, "They shall walk with me in white, for they are worthy." Was it then for nothing that God made the snowdrops?

THE END

LITTLE VIOLET

CHAPTER
ONE

THE LAW OF THE VIOLET

Oh, how very dull it was! The poor little girl had to lie in bed all day because she had taken a bad cold; her mama said that was the only way to get rid of it. She had counted all the folds of the curtains and examined every turn of the green twisting pattern of the paper on the wall. She had looked at the little ornaments on the mantelpiece until they seemed to turn into all manner of forms. She had been playing with her pillow until her arms ached. And now her head ached too and her eyes were tired. She wished very much that she had something to amuse herself.

Poor little Violet! How glad she was when she heard a quick, bounding step on the stairs and her sister Ellen came in to see how the little prisoner was getting on.

"Oh, Ellen, I'm so glad—it is so dull!"

"Of course it is, you poor little thing," said kind, bright Ellen as she threw herself onto the end of the bed, tossed off her little black hat, and shook back the curls from her merry face.

"And you look so happy," said Violet mournfully.

"I've got no cold," Ellen replied rather mischievously.

"Well, I can't help mine."

"No, I never said you could. But really, Violet, I'm very sorry, for Aunt Charlotte has sent over to ask us to tea tonight, and Mama says you can't go."

Violet's face grew very long.

"Who's going?" she asked dismally.

"Papa and Mama, and Francis and I. Tom has got to stay at home and study tonight."

"Oh, dear!"

"I'm so sorry. Shall I stay at home with you?" said Ellen half hesitatingly, which showed the strong effort she spent in making such a proposal.

"Oh, no, no, no!" and Violet shook her head very decidedly.

"Well, I'll lend you 'Cheerful Annie' or some of my books."

"No, not that, because I don't feel cheerful at all."

"All the more reason why you should want it— it's beautiful, I think."

"Is it?" Violet turned her head quickly, and Ellen did not see that tears were falling on the soft, white pillow. She only noticed that her sister was very quiet, and thinking she was sleepy, she got off the bed, drew the curtain across the

69

window, and left the little girl alone.

Then Violet had a regular fit of crying over her disappointment, which made her eyes ache more than ever. She thought Ellen need hardly have come up to tantalize her with the thought of the pleasure which she was not to share. Rather hard thoughts about Ellen passed through the little maiden's mind as she wondered if Ellen had told her on purpose to tease her.

Presently Violet's mama came in to see her, and that cheered the little girl directly. The touch of Mama's hand on Violet's aching forehead, the pleasant way in which Mama settled the pillow and smoothed the clothes, and the kind, cheerful tones of Mama's sweet voice could not fail to do good to her little daughter.

But Mama's quick eye was not long in discovering that something had been fretting Violet, and she asked what it was.

"Only—only," and Violet choked down a sob, "it's so dull, and I want to go to Aunt Charlotte's tonight."

"That is impossible, love. You will only make those poor eyes more burning and uncomfortable if you cry about it."

"But, Mama, Cousin Charlie is to be there."

"Well, some night he will come to visit us also."

"It's so horrid lying up here all day," grumbled Violet.

"Well, my child, we all know that colds are not pleasant things, but the only thing to cure them is patience, to be taken in large doses."

Violet smiled. "Mama, I think patience is a most horrid dose; it doesn't agree with me, I'm certain."

Mrs. Thornton shook her head. "You don't agree with it yet, my little girl, but before you are done with it, you will get to like it."

"Have you, Mama?"

"Yes, darling."

"But isn't it much more *pleasant* to make a great fuss and toss about and cry when you don't like a thing than to lie still and be *patient?*"

"I don't find it so now, Violet; it is better to let patience have her perfect work." With these words Mrs. Thornton stooped down and kissed her little girl's cheek. Violet looked into that calm, sweet face and wondered if anybody in all the world was as good as her mama.

"You are better tonight, dear. I think your stay in Bedfordshire has done you good," Mrs. Thornton said after a moment or two as she stroked Violet's dark hair back from her forehead.

"Oh, yes, Mama, I'm much better; and I do so want to get up."

"Well, supposing I say that you may get up and come down to the library to make tea for

Tom tonight, will you sit very quietly while he studies?"

"Oh, you dear, good Mama, I am so glad! To be sure, I will be quiet like a little mouse; and Ellen has promised to lend me her new book."

"Very well then, my child, I will send nurse to you, but you must not sit up very late. Now I must go and get ready. Good night, dear Violet."

Soon after the whole party had gone, a funny little figure, well wrapped up, came into the library, where a bright fire was burning. Tom Thornton was there up to his elbows in large books, running the fingers of his one hand through his hair and supporting his forehead with the other hand. Violet knew this position always meant that he was at something more difficult than usual.

But intent as he was upon his work, no sooner did the young student see his little sister coming into the room than he rose. Coming forward, he said cheerily, "Well, Mouse, so you've come to spend the evening with me. How's the cold?"

"Better," croaked Violet in a very hoarse voice. Then as he pulled a comfortable armchair up to the fire for her and brought the little table to her side, she coiled herself up and put her feet on the fender.

"Now, Tom, I've promised Mama not to disturb you, and so be very quiet indeed while you go back to those big, stupid-looking books."

"Poor little Mouse. Well, I will work on until teatime, and then I'll be at your service for a game of chess or anything else you like."

"Oh, thank you, good old Tom."

"Or look here, will this do better? I got them on my way home tonight, and this little white jug for you to put them in," and Tom placed a bunch of purple violets on the little table beside her.

"Oh, Tom, for me? And this dear little white

Parian jug—what made you think of it?"

"Well, it was natural that the sight of the little violets should remind me of the poor, small Violet we had shut up at home, and so it was not such an extraordinary thing that, having some coppers in my pocket, I should exchange them for this little bunch to brighten you up. There now, I must go back to work."

So Tom returned to his books, and Violet's fingers were very busy arranging her little purple namesakes, delighting herself in their delicious perfume, their rich color, and their soft green leaves. When every violet was in its proper place, the water was put in, and the ends of the stalks were thrown into the fire, the little girl leaned back in her chair and looked at her work with great satisfaction.

While she was thinking of many things connected with them, she was startled by the entrance of the servant with tea—she could hardly believe that it was an hour since she came down. As Tom shut his books with a decided bang, which told that his work was finished for the present, she looked up joyfully, saying, "Tom, I'm glad I couldn't go to Aunt Charlotte's. You'd have been very dull without me."

Tom did not tell her that, had it not been for her, he should have gone to Aunt Charlotte's as soon as he had finished his work. He only smiled at her across the table, admired her violets, and piled up all his books.

Tea went on merrily, and when it was finished, Tom got out the chess board. Soon they were deeply engaged in a game, but Violet's brain was not very clear, and she made such desperate mistakes that she was soon beaten; then, with a great yawn, she declared that she could not play anymore.

"No, I don't think you can," said Tom kindly.

"Well, now then, Tom, draw your chair near the fire and let's have a talk. It isn't often I get you all to myself, and I want to ask you so many things."

"Well," said her brother as he seized the poker and began to vigorously stir the fire, "what's the first?"

"Well, I've been thinking what an odd thing it was to call me Violet. It never struck me until tonight. What made them do it?"

A sad shade passed over Tom's face as he answered, "It was Rose's wish."

"Poor Rose who died just after I was born?"

"Yes, she was very ill when you were born, and when Papa asked her what she would like you to be called, she answered, 'I should like you to have a Violet when your Rose is dead.' And Papa said it should be so, especially as everyone declared your eyes were violet, which they aren't, you know, not one single bit."

"No, gray-green is what Francis calls them. But, Tom—"

"Well?"

"I'm not like a violet anyway."

"How now? What odd fancy is coming up now?" asked Tom, laughing.

"Don't laugh, Tom. I've been thinking names should suit, and all the rest do, but mine doesn't."

"What do you mean?"

"Why, you're Tom; anyone would know that because there's something so kind and strong and jolly about the name."

"Don't talk slang, Violet," said her brother, shaking his head with an air of mock gravity.

"And then there's Ellen," she continued, unheeding his interruption. "She's so bright and merry, her name's just right; and Francis, free and mischievous—but shrewd; and Rose, so beautiful and pure and loved by everyone, and dying away like

79

the flower. But I'm not a bit like my name. I ought to be very beautiful and shy and have people come to search for me like some great treasure."

"You queer little thing," said Tom, looking around into her demure little face.

"No, Tom, now you're laughing, and I'm quite grave. I mean it."

"Well, shall I tell you what I think about it?"

"Yes."

"My idea of your little namesake flower is different from yours. I always fancy it more like a little German rhyme which I am very fond of—

> Learn from it with pure endeavor,
> Good to do, and nothing say.

To me, the law of the violet seems to be, do as much good as possible in the little space appointed to it."

Violet bent forward, her eyes full of eager

excitement. Tom, seeing her look of pleasure, went on. "When one comes near a bank of violets, one perceives them long before seeing the flowers, because of their delicious aroma. There are some people who are always doing little kind actions and thoughtful things for others, like Mama for instance, that seem to do good in the same way."

"Oh, Tom, I see, I see—go on!"

"I haven't much more to say, Violet," said Tom gravely, "only there's one other thought comes to me of the little flower glorifying its Maker by its life of gladness, that purple glowing color, and that delicious fragrance doing their work and fulfilling the exact mission for which they were made, with—

> A work of lowly love to do
> For the Lord on whom they wait.

Am I too fanciful for you?"

Violet's eyes were glistening with pleasure.

"No, no. Those lines were from the hymn you like so much, and I shall learn it by next Sunday."

Tom was gazing thoughtfully into the fire and hardly heeded her words.

"Violet," he said after a few moments' pause, "I have not been saying my own words to you; I have only been reviewing a talk I once had with Rose about those flowers."

Violet knew how he had loved Rose and how seldom he mentioned her to anyone, so she showed her sympathy by only laying her hand on his and whispering, "I should like to be the kind of Violet she would have had me be."

"I understand," said Tom heartily. Then, looking up at the little white-faced clock ticking away on the mantelpiece, he added, "It's only half an hour until prayer time. Shall I read you Sir Walter Scott's 'Lady of the Lake' for a little while?"

Violet eagerly assented, and the time passed quickly away in this pleasant occupation. At half past nine the servants came in, and Tom read a chapter from the Bible. His little sister liked to listen to his grave, sweet voice, and she thought he was thinking of the violet work when he chose for their evening portion the chapter which describes that "charity that seeketh not her own."

She went to bed directly after prayers were over, but as she bade Tom good night, she whispered, "I shan't forget, I've been so happy, Tom."

CHAPTER
TWO

A TORN FROCK

A week passed away, during which time Violet lost her cold and made some advance in her newly discovered work.

Tom found a pair of gloves, that he had left in holes, neatly mended and laid beside his hat on the hall table.

Mr. Thornton, when he returned from his afternoon round of visits to his patients (for he was a doctor), was greeted in his study by the sight of a blazing fire and his slippers toasting before it.

Francis, who was rigging a small ship, was

delighted to find a new sail that Ellen had promised to make for him. Although he had forgotten as usual, there it was, lying with his tools—of exactly the shape and size which he required. He could not imagine who had put it there, knowing that Violet hated work and never willingly took a needle into her hand.

Mrs. Thornton could not understand how it was that when she went to look through the boys' clothes, she found nothing wanting a button or string.

It was Saturday afternoon, and the little girls had a half-holiday.

Papa had given Violet a new book, which she had kept as a treat for that day. Finding no one in the dining room, she took possession of a large armchair near the fire and was soon deep in the delights of her story. Presently Ellen came dancing into the room. "Violet! Tom says he can take us out for a good long walk. Will you come and get ready?"

Violet sprang from her seat and ran off after her sister. She knew the pleasure of a walk with Tom. It was none of the dry, stupid "constitutionals" as Papa called them, but a good long ramble. They would leave the town with its noise, smoke, dirt, and bustle behind them and scramble up the breezy hillsides through furze and gorse bushes, not heeding the brambles and briars in the way and never stopping till they had reached the free open country and were breathing pure, fresh air.

"Hadn't we better change our frocks, Ellen? You know these are our best," said Violet, looking down at their neat, checked frocks of blue and white.

"Oh, no, I shan't change mine," said Ellen. "It's too much trouble; I'll take care of it. What a stupid little fidget you are, Violet," she added as she saw her sister quietly unfastening hers and replacing it with one of dark brown tweed.

"I shall feel happier in this," said Violet, smiling good-humoredly. In a few minutes the two little girls joined their brother, who was waiting for them in the hall.

It was a walk after Violet's own heart, and it seemed doubly pleasant because she had been shut up for so many days.

Ellen would have enjoyed it also, had it not been that she tore her dress in climbing over a fence. The little girls had a rule that they were to mend whatever they tore, so the rest of her walk was clouded with the idea of the long piece of work she would have to do, and the hour that would be taken from her playtime for the purpose.

As they were taking off their frocks on their return, Violet asked, "Ellen, wouldn't it be better to mend your frock now and have it done?"

"Very well," said Ellen, "and will you read a story

to me while I do it?"

Violet would rather have gone back to her comfortable armchair and her own book, but on second thought, she agreed. Having found a story, sat down beside her sister and began reading. Ellen, who after a long hunt had discovered her needle and cotton, set to work upon the unfortunate frock.

But both sisters started up in a few minutes as their ears caught the sound of carriage wheels coming up to the door.

"It's Uncle Temple, and Ronald is with him, oh, joy, joy!" cried Violet, throwing down her book and running out of the room. Ellen quickly followed her, and they met their uncle and their sailor cousin in the hall. Their cousin had just returned from his first voyage.

"Well, little nieces, you see I've brought Ronald to see you. Is he grown out of all recollection? Is Papa in, or Mama?"

"Yes, in the drawing room," said Ellen, leading the way, while Violet and Ronald followed more slowly. Violet was looking half shyly, but with very admiring eyes, upon her cousin's bronzed face.

"Well, Miss Violet, you'll know me again," he said, laughing.

"I was looking to see if I did know you," she answered, "but now that you laugh, you're just the same as ever."

"And I suppose you are as idle and mischievous as you can be," said Ronald.

"Not quite," Violet replied, shaking her head. "I dare say you've had heaps of adventures."

"Loads. I'll tell you all about them. And Papa's come over to bring you and Ellen and Francis back to the rectory to stay till Monday."

"Oh, what fun, what fun!" cried Violet.

"Ellen, do you hear? We are to go back to the rectory to spend Ronald's first Sunday at home."

"Oh, then I must go and finish my frock!" said Ellen, but somehow she did not go, and minute after minute slipped by. Ronald's stories grew more and more entertaining, and Ellen forgot all about the mending.

At last her uncle turned around and said, "Ellen, my dear, your mama says you and Francis and Violet may come over till Monday. Will you run and get ready?"

Ellen started to her feet. *Oh, my frock, my frock!* she thought, *and it's such a long tear! Why, I never should have worn it. If Mama knows it is torn, she will not let me go in this old brown one. Where can Violet be? Oh, she might come and help me!* She sprang up the stairs two steps at a time until she had reached their room. There she found Violet quietly locking the little bag into which nurse had packed their things, and the blue dress lay on the bed.

"Oh, Violet, Violet, what shall I do? That horrid

dress—where is my cotton? Quick, quick, I will cobble it up some way."

Violet smiled, and the next moment Ellen discovered the rent neatly mended and the dress all

ready to be worn.

"Oh, you dear, good, little thing, did you give it to nurse? Was that why you slipped away from Ronald's stories? They were such fun, I *could* not come. I must run and thank nurse."

"I did it," said Violet, coloring very much.

"You! You mean to say you've darned it all like this? Oh, Violet, what a pet you are!" Ellen threw her arms around her sister's neck and gave her a hearty kiss.

CHAPTER
THREE

TWENTY-TWO SHILLINGS

We must not linger over the pleasant Sunday the children spent at their uncle's rectory, which was about four miles out of the town.

Ronald was an only son and the joy and delight of that quiet home. His return was the signal for universal gladness. His cousins were like brothers and sisters to him, and until they came over to share in the rejoicings, he did not feel that it was a proper homecoming. But it would make our story too long to dwell on their happiness, so we must hasten over the next two days and join them in the dining room at home on Monday evening.

Violet was giving Tom an account of a class of very small children she had taught, and Francis was hard at work upon his ship, making some improvements that Ronald had suggested.

At last Mr. Thornton joined them, looking very weary, as if something had tried him. He threw himself into the armchair, stroked Violet's hair, and then gazed silently and thoughtfully into her face.

"What's the matter, Papa?"

"I was thinking what a dreadful thing it is to see a little child suffer pain," replied her father gravely. "I visited a little boy this afternoon who can never move from his couch except to be carried to bed. I do not think he can live very long, but even if he does, he will always live in pain. His parents are not rich enough to give him many necessary things. His mother has to teach music all day, and his father is engaged in an office in the city. Poor little Edward, who has no brothers or sisters, is entirely left to the charge of a servant maid. When I went in today, I found him crying from loneliness and pain, and when I asked why he cried, he answered, 'I can't help it. I've got nothing else to do.' "

"Oh, Papa," cried Ellen, "may we lend him some picture books and things?"

Mr. Thornton smiled. "Yes, you shall, dear, if you like it."

"And may we go to see him" she added eagerly.

"Yes, certainly. That will do him more good than anything," said her father kindly.

Accordingly, on the following day, Mr. Thornton took the two little girls with him to visit little Edward Sharpe. They brought him out of their stores a picture book and a puzzle, with some oranges as a present from Mama.

Edward was shy at first, but this soon wore off and he greatly enjoyed their visit. For a few days

Ellen went regularly to see him, as the house where he lived was close to her home; but by degrees her visits became fewer and far between and at length ceased altogether. She began to find it harder work than she had thought to give up so many of her play hours to visit a sick, fretful, restless boy who required constant amusement.

Poor little Edward missed her very much the first day that she did not come, but on the second day, instead of Miss Ellen, Miss Violet came in, bringing a little bunch of flowers for him.

"I've brought a storybook too. Shall I read to you a little bit?" she asked kindly.

"Oh, please," said Edward, his whole face brightening.

So Violet read to him and tried to soothe his pain through the long hours of that bright, sunshiny afternoon. She did not tell him that to come brighten and cheer him in his loneliness, she had given up a pleasant drive with her Aunt Charlotte. But he, for whose sake she did this kind deed, looked with pleasure upon her work, and it did not lose its reward.

"Can you sing?" asked little Edward suddenly when she had finished the story and laid down the book.

"Yes, I sing enough to amuse myself. Sometimes I sing when I am all by myself."

"Do you think you could sing me something? I do so love music, but Mother's piano is downstairs, so I never hear it. When I hear music, it seems to lessen the pain."

"I will try and sing then," said Violet. "What shall it be?"

"Oh, a hymn. Something soft."

So Violet went through several of her own favorites, and the look of pain on the little fellow's thin flushed face became less intense, and in some of the last verses he tried to join.

"Thank you," he said when she stood up to go away. "Please come again. Miss Ellen's very kind, but I like you best."

Violet did not repeat this to Ellen, but she went on visiting little Edward whenever she could, trying to think of every little thing she could do to throw some brightness into his sad life.

She had found plenty of ways now of imitating her little namesake flower, and had

> Learned from it with pure endeavor
> Good to do, and nothing say.

Just at this time her old nurse was taken ill, and Violet found that there were a great many ways in which she could help her mama to nurse her. She would sit for hours with unwearied patience by her bedside, watching to get whatever she wanted, to give her medicine and food at the right times, and

to make herself useful as well as she could.

When old Rachel began to get better, no one was so careful of her or so willing to attend upon her as Miss Violet. The old woman herself said,

"Not even dear Miss Rose, had she been spared, could have been more kind to me, nor taken more care of me, than that dear, bright child. No, not if she'd been my own daughter could she have done better for me. The Lord bless her for it!"

Mr. Thornton was very pleased with his little daughter's thoughtfulness. On the day that old Rachel came down for the first time, Violet's father told her she deserved a doctor's fee for making her well. At the same minute he laid down half a sovereign on the table before her.

"Oh, Papa," she said, blushing profusely, "I can't take this. Of course I liked to be with Rachel, and I can't take this money. Please don't."

Mr. Thornton stooped down, parted the hair off her forehead, and kissed her.

"I don't give it you, love, because you have nursed Rachel, but because I am so pleased to see the thoughtful kindness you have shown lately in so many ways. You are my own little fireside Violet. Now put your money away into your purse and do what you like with it."

Violet looked up, all radiant with joy at this unsought praise. Then she put the money into her purse and thought with delight of how much it would further a little scheme she had in her head.

With quick, bounding steps she ran upstairs to her little drawer and counted her money.

"Fifteen shillings, and Papa's ten make twenty-five. Only five more needed, and then I can get it," she said to herself joyously. "It will be only a little one, but much better than nothing."

One afternoon a few days after this, when Violet was busily practicing a difficult piece of music, Francis suddenly came into the room, looking very troubled and almost crying. He took no notice of Violet, only walked over towards the window, and threw himself into a chair.

After a moment or two he cried out hastily," Do stop that now, Violet!"

Violet got up, closed the piano, and went over to him.

"What is it, Francis. What's the matter? Do tell me."

A low, half-smothered sob was her brother's only reply as he hid his face in the window curtain.

"Francis, please tell me," Violet whispered, bending her face down close to his.

"You won't care; it's nothing to you," he answered in a low, husky voice.

"Yes, it is, it must be, if it hurts you. Speak to me, Francis."

"Can I trust you? Will you not tell?" he asked, hurriedly raising his head for one moment and gazing earnestly into her face.

"No, I won't tell," said Violet firmly.

"Well, look here. You know the fellows said—that

is—they all think I'm so careful and steady and all that, and they made me keep the money for the cricket club. I was collecting it yesterday, and like a fool, I put it all into my waistcoat pocket, and it has a hole. I've dropped it all—every halfpenny—and tomorrow it will be wanted, and I've not got it."

"But can't you tell them you've dropped it?" asked Violet after a minute's silence.

"No, what good will that do? The last fellow who kept it said he'd dropped it, and they all knew he'd spent it."

"But you haven't; surely they'll believe your words," said Violet eagerly.

"There's no saying. They'll be savage at the money being lost, and I daren't ask Papa, because he gave me a pound not long ago."

"How much is it?" asked Violet.

"Twenty-two shillings I've got to make up; thirty it was I lost, but I've got eight of my own. I say, Violet, can you lend me some? I know you've been saving."

A quick thrill of disappointment ran through Violet's mind. If she gave her money to Francis, what would become of her own little cherished scheme? No, no, she could not bear the penalty of Francis' carelessness. No, she could not help him. Then she looked in his miserable face and watched him eagerly trying to read her decision. Then she thought, *"Christ pleased not himself," and I want to be like Him. It will be for my own pleasure that I keep the money for the purpose for which I have saved it, and though it is to give pleasure to another person as well, I think it must be more right for me to help my own brother first.*

But it was very hard. No one knew the battle that went on in Violet's mind for those few short minutes before she stooped down and kissed Francis' cheek, whispering, "I can give it to you. I'll run and get it." Away she went to fetch her cherished savings. She returned very quickly and emptied her little purse on the table. There was Papa's bright half-sovereign, two half-crowns from Uncle Temple, and all her own allowances of six-pence a week for several weeks back. With some other coins besides, she counted out twenty-two shillings, and pushed them over to Francis, who could hardly believe his good fortune.

"Well, Violet, you're first rate. Why, you little miser, how came you by such a hoard? And to have kept it so quiet—but really, I am very much obliged. There, you see, I don't want it all; you have three shillings left. I shan't forget it, Violet. I only hope I shall be able to do you a good turn some day." Francis jingled the money in his hand and capered about the room with joy. "I'll go and pay it out to Fraser directly," he cried, "and then it will be safe for this time. Hurrah for you, Violet! In the future, I'll know who to come to in a scrape."

"And please, if you'll leave your waistcoat on the chair upstairs, I'll mend it," Violet cried after him as he banged the door behind him.

When Francis was gone, Violet slowly took up the three shillings that were left, looked at them long and silently, then dropped them into her purse. "I must begin again," she said to herself mournfully. "I was so near the end, and now I must begin all over again."

With her head upon the table and her hands over her eyes, Violet tried vainly to drive away those refractory tears. She did not hear a footstep in the room, nor perceive that anyone had come in, until a hand was gently laid on her shoulder, and Tom's kind voice said, "Violet crying! Why, what's the matter?"

"Nothing," sobbed the little girl, but the kind voice of sympathy only made her tears flow the faster.

Tom knelt beside her and put one arm around

her, drawing her head onto his shoulder.

"Don't tell me it is nothing," he said gently, putting his hand on her forehead. "Has it anything to say to the good deed you have done for Francis? I have just met him in tearing spirits about it, and he told me how kind you've been. Is that what you're crying for, Violet?"

"Oh, Tom, I know it's wrong and selfish of me to be crying; only, I can't help it. Don't tell Francis, please, promise you won't."

"I won't if you'll tell me all about it," he answered, smiling.

"Well, I don't like to. I don't want to talk about it, but—"

"You may trust me," said Tom. "I'm as safe as a lock and key."

"And will you understand and not think that I mean what I don't?" asked Violet rather anxiously.

"I'll try," replied Tom.

"Well, you see, little Edward Sharpe does love music so much. It always does him good and seems to help him to bear the pain better, so I've been thinking—that is, I've been saving to get him a little musical box that would play him little tunes when he is lonely. I found I could get just a small one with three tunes for thirty shillings, and I had gotten all but five. I know it was selfish, and thinking most of my own pleasure, not to be willing and ready for Francis to have it, but I won't cry anymore; I'm done now," and she looked with a brave, happy smile into his face.

Tom only answered by giving her a kiss and whispering, "Well done, little Violet!" Then he added, "Now run off and put on your things to come for a walk with me."

Need we say how gladly Violet obeyed him?

CHAPTER FOUR

VIOLET'S BIRTHDAY

" Many happy returns of the day, my little girl," said Mr. Thornton as he entered the dining room one bright April morning about three weeks after the events of our last chapter.

Violet ran forward to meet him, and he put into her hands a beautifully bound book that she had long wanted. She thanked him with great delight and then showed him the pretty work box Mama had given her and a nice little inkstand that Ellen and Francis had jointly surprised her with, though we suspect that Ellen had most to say to its purchase.

"I'm rich, Papa, am I not?" she asked delightedly.

"No, not until I have given you mine," whispered Tom, who was sitting beside her.

"Well, and what are you going to do today? What is to be your birthday treat?" asked her father.

"I don't know, Papa. I've got a holiday, and I've plenty to do."

"Yes, but what is to be the great treat?" Mrs. Thornton asked. "Cousin Charlie is coming this evening, and Uncle Temple and Ronald are coming to spend the day tomorrow."

Violet sprang from her chair with a cry of pleasure. "Oh, you dear, good Mama, what a treat! And Tom, do you think we can take that long scrambling walk over Ferny Hill and round through the woods? We should get quantities of flowers, and it would be so lovely. Oh, do let us!"

"Well, we'll try," said Tom.

Uncle Temple and Roland arrived soon after

breakfast, bringing Violet a beautiful canary in a nice cage, which seemed to put the finishing stroke to her delight.

A real live pet to be taken care of—a little bird to sing to her, to learn to know her, and to be her very, very own. It seemed too good to be true, but there was Master Dick hopping about on his perch and looking as happy and important as a new cage and the brightest of yellow coats could make him.

It was a matter of great debate where the cage was to be hung, but at last it was decided that the best place would be in Violet's own old nursery, where Rachel now spent her life, and Violet almost all her spare hours.

At twelve o'clock the party was to have started on their expedition, taking their luncheon with them, but their bright hopes were dashed by April's treacherous weather! The sky clouded over, and when they were all assembled in the hall, they discovered that it was pouring rain. Violet's face clouded as she saw the state of things, and with an impatient sigh she turned to Ronald, saying, "It's always the way, when one has thought of anything pleasant. I do hate April weather."

"Oh, for shame, Violet. It's your own month!" exclaimed Ronald.

"If it weren't for April showers and April sunshine, where would be the violets?" asked Tom.

And Ellen added:

> None of all the wreaths ye prize
> But was nursed by weeping skies,
> Keen March winds and April showers
> Braced the roots, embalmed the flowers.

"Oh, bother," said Francis, "don't quote poetry at us."

"Do you think it will clear up, Tom?" asked Violet anxiously.

"Not at present; perhaps after luncheon."

Violet turned around and walked into the dining room with a very discontented look on her face. But in a moment or two she came back with her own sunny smile. "It's no good letting the rain waste all our morning. Ellen, let us take off our things, and then we will all have a good game at bagatelle. Ronald, you must be on my side. I won't have you as an enemy."

She seemed to come like a sunbeam amongst them, clearing up the shower, for everyone's face grew contented. In a short time they were all deeply engaged in their game.

At the end of the first game, Violet slipped away, and Tom followed her. He found her cloaked and bonneted in the hall, looking for her umbrella.

"Where are you off to?" he asked.

"Oh, Tom, I thought I could go and see Edward for a little while before dinner and take him this jelly which Mama has had made for him."

"Well, look here, Violet," said Tom, opening the door of the little room where he generally studied and leading her into it. "You have not had my birthday present yet," and he put a little square parcel into her hands.

With hasty fingers she unfastened it, and then a cry of "Tom!—oh, how could you?" burst from her as she discovered a music box.

"Will that do?" Tom asked kindly.

Violet's eyes glistened with pleasure, but at length, looking up with a start, she asked, "Tom, do you mean this for me?"

"I mean you to do exactly as you like with it," he answered, smiling. "It is my birthday present to you."

"Then I may give it to Edward as my own present?"

"Most certainly."

"Oh, Tom, you dear, good brother! How shall

116

I thank you?"

"By enjoying your visit to Edward," he replied, and then he sent her off on her happy errand.

She found the little boy in greater pain than usual and very tearful.

"Oh, Miss Violet, it's no good. I've been trying to be patient, and trying to bear it, and it isn't any good," he said sorrowfully.

"Don't say that, dear Edward," whispered his little comforter. "God will make you patient if you ask Him. You know we can't do anything until He helps us."

Edward smiled faintly, but then as Violet drew forth the little box, put it on the table and wound it up, his look changed to one of delighted pleasure. When the little fairy notes—so sweet, so clear, and so ringing—fell on his ear, he half started up, then leaned forward with his finger on his lips, and at last covered his face with his hands and cried.

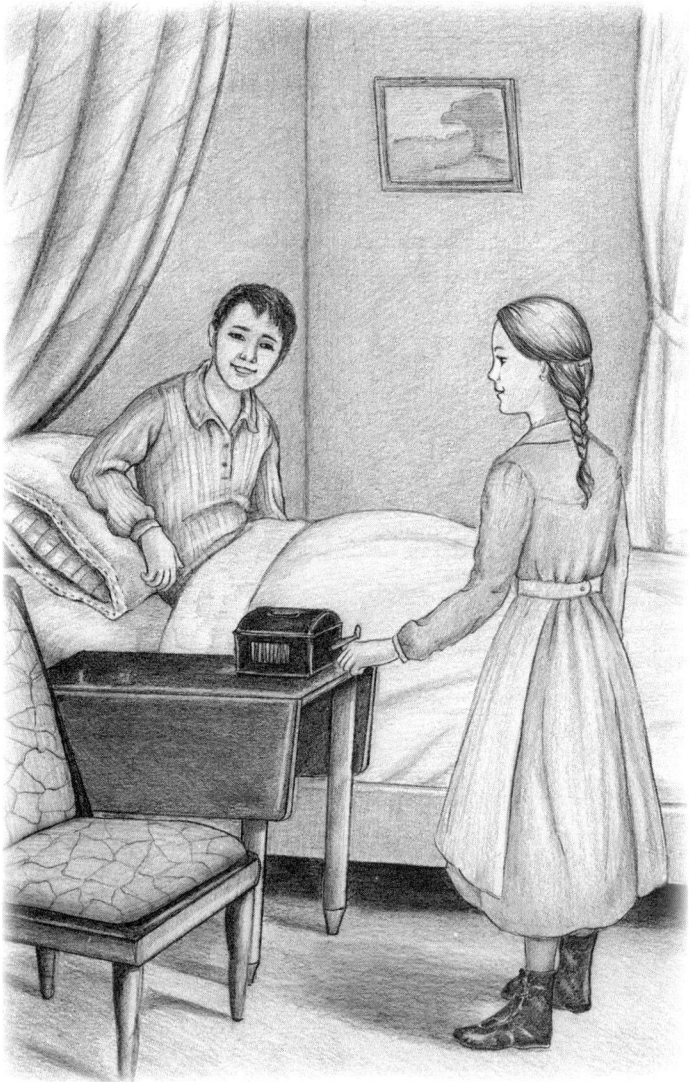

"Don't you like it?" asked Violet, a little disappointed.

"Oh, it's like what I've dreamed about! It's like—oh, Miss Violet, will it ever play again?"

"Yes, there goes another tune, 'Home, sweet home.' "

"Oh, it seems to rest me so! Will you bring it again? Please do. I will be good if you'll bring it again. Indeed, I will."

"I've brought it for you altogether, Edward. You are to keep it always so that you may never be without music," she replied.

"For *me?*—for *me?*—for my very own?" cried the little fellow eagerly.

"Yes," said Violet, almost as pleased as he was.

"Oh, what will Mother say? Miss Violet, I never will cry anymore."

Violet wished that Tom were there to share her joy, but as it was nearly dinnertime, she could not stay any longer with the happy little boy. After watching his delight for a few moments, and then showing him the way to wind up his box, she left him, no longer fretful, tearful, and lonely. Knowing that Edward was comforted and delighted with his new treasure, Violet walked home, her heart echoing the words of Him who said, "It is more blessed to give than to receive."

The afternoon was fine, and directly after luncheon the young party set out for Ferny Hill. The expedition was as prosperous as bright sunshine, lovely scenery, and happy hearts could make it, and the birthday evening passed away delightfully. Let us leave our little Violet in the full enjoyment of it, knowing that He who has taught her to love Him and to give her heart to Him will keep her and bless her to the end of her life. And she, happy in her quiet home, will continue to be the bright little flower she loves to imitate, cheering and comforting silently all who come within her influence, and filling her own little spot in God's earth rightly and wisely, being glad in her heart because she has been given

> A work of lowly love to do
> For the Lord on whom she waits.

THE END

OTHER EARLY CLASSICS PRINTED BY CHRISTIAN AID MINISTRIES

THE SHEPHERD OF BETHLEHEM
A.L.O.E.

An excellent classic tale originally published in 1877. A small, motley audience listens as a clergyman lectures on the life of David the shepherd-king.
366 pages | $19.95

THE HERMIT'S CHRISTMAS
DAVID DE FOREST BURRELL

An intriguing story set in the Middle Ages, probably toward the end of the Crusades. As a hermit teaches his visitors the true meaning of Christmas, he is forced to examine his own heart. Originally published in 1912.
49 pages | $9.99

SOPHY CLAYMORE
A.L.O.E.

A blind orphan girl, adopted by a kind man, flounders in her faith in God. Poverty haunts their footsteps until an unexpected answer turns up, and Sophy learns to trust at last. Originally printed in 1870.
64 pages | $9.99

Continued on next page

NELLY'S DARK DAYS
SARAH SMITH

Young Nelly does not remember her father before he was enslaved in the savage grip of strong drink. Only when he turns to God for deliverance do Nelly's dark days become bright. Originally printed in 1870.
112 pages | $11.99

THE WOODCUTTER OF GUTECH
W. H. KINGSTON

When the Reformation sweeps across Germany, a woodcutter and his grandchildren hear the story of Jesus' sacrifice on the cross and realize that salvation does not come through performing penances and confessing to the priests. They believe the Gospel and seek to follow God's Word. Read how the woodcutter lives out nonresistance in daily life and through suffering. Originally printed in 1873.
96 pages | $11.99

SAVED BY LOVE
EMMA LESLIE

Through an orphan friend's love, words, and example, Elfie learns about a loving Father in heaven and is saved from her lonely, wretched existence on the streets of London. Originally printed in 1895.
136 pages | $12.99